Sensitive Sam

Visits the Dentist

This lively story includes a variety of worthwhile resources for kids' dental visits, from caring adults that know exactly what to do. Endorsed by dentists and child development experts.

Marla Roth-Fisch

Sensitive Sam Visits the Dentist

All marketing and publishing rights guaranteed to and reserved by:

FUTURE HORIZONS INC.

721 W Abram St, Arlington, TX 76013
800-489-0727 (toll free)
817-277-0727 (local)
817-277-2270 (fax)

E-mail: *info@fhautism.com*
www.fhautism.com

ISBN: 978-0-986067-30-3

Advance Praise for
Sensitive Sam Visits the Dentist

"Having a good first experience with going to the dentist will help a child with autism tolerate the dentist. This book will help children on the spectrum better understand visits to the dentist."

– Dr. Temple Grandin
prominent advocate for the autistic community, animal
expert, and the subject of an award-winning film

"What could be more difficult for a child with Sensory Processing Disorder (SPD) than a visit to the dentist? Even the thought of the appointment can send some children into a meltdown.

Now, finally, there is a book for children that moms and dads can read to and with their child at home before they go to the dentist. When the story is read over and over again, a child will internalize the message: 'I am happy now, my dental exam, a breeze. And it's time for Mom, sis, and I to leave.'

I highly recommend this entertaining and pragmatic approach to increasing the comfort of children with SPD when visiting their dentists! Happy teeth cleaning to all!"

– Dr. Lucy Jane Miller
founder of the first nationwide comprehensive
Sensory Processing Disorder research program

Acknowledgments

Many thanks to all the "sensational" contributors for their personal stories, solutions, and grassroots advocacy! They always put the children first.

I'd also like to express my everlasting gratitude to the leading experts in the field of Sensory Processing Disorder (SPD) and autism, who have conducted countless hours of research, generated worldwide awareness of SPD, and dedicated themselves to "the cause."

We wouldn't be where we are today without them.

Many thanks go to the dentists and hygienists for their expertise in helping special-needs children have the best dental experience ever by providing an invaluable "Special Tips Section." They all realize the importance of providing preventive treatments and developing strong relationships with their special-needs patients and families.

We couldn't have accomplished this without the talented editors and artists who polished this manuscript and the outstanding publisher and staff who understand the power of disseminating informative resources.

This acknowledgment would not be complete without mentioning the backbone of my inspiration—the love and support of my family.

Foreword

In her marvelous second book, Marla Roth-Fisch explores a part of the body that experiences sensations from the very beginning of life–the mouth. The mouth is the source of nutrition, speech, and linguistic register. But just as the mouth gives and receives so much pleasure from food, kissing, and smiling, it can also be a mysterious place–dark, unseen, and sometimes painful.

Teachers, parents, and dentists can do a great service for children by demystifying the mouth and keeping it healthy and thriving. Topics suggested by the National Institute of Dental and Craniofacial Research from the National Institutes of Health *(www.nidcr.nih.gov)* suggest six major topics for discussion and learning by posing six questions for children: *(a)* What do mouths do? *(b)* What's inside the mouth? *(c)* What's tooth decay? *(d)* What lives inside your mouth? *(e)* What keeps your mouth healthy? *(f)* What steps can you take to maintain a healthy mouth?

While children and their parents or guardians are waiting for the dentist, the parts of the mouth can be identified–lips, tongue, teeth, and gums–and this can help clarify the language that will be used in the dental office. For young children, practicing "Open wide!" with the mouth (and eyes, hands, and arms) can be fun. Another conversation would be to think of all the things that get brushed: hair, pets, paints ... even the street sweeper uses brushes to clean the streets!

And what about germs? What does the child know about germs that can make people sick and how to get rid of them?

Another topic to consider is the role of the dentist and her (or his) staff as helpers to keep people healthy. Each thing the helpers do makes children healthy and keeps them from being in pain, so children can play and learn without having any pain in their teeth. What are some fun things the child likes to do? Parents could bring in props for these conversations–photos of the child playing could prompt the question, "What would happen if you had a toothache at the beach?" This serves as both a distraction and an opportunity for learning and demystifying some of the things the dentist might do, such as using a tiny mirror to see better in the small spaces or putting little cotton balls in the mouth so it won't be so slippery!

Ultimately, it is the parents who set the tone for dental health. If they are fearful and negative, it is likely that their children will be, too. However, if the parents seem upbeat and speak positively about their dental experiences ("I didn't have any cavities–probably because I don't eat candy on a regular basis"), their children will follow suit.

Being a positive role model is the best investment parents can make in the vitality of their children's most wonderful mouths–for more kisses, eating, and talking!

Carrie Rothstein-Fisch, PhD
Professor of Educational Psychology and Counseling
California State University, Northridge

It is time to go; we leave the
house about ten 'til four,
My feet hit the floor dragging
and soon we are out the door.

Baby sister, Mom, and I pile
into the car, and my Mom
says that the dentist's office
is close by, not too far.

My dental visit came around so fast that I've forgotten what my dentist did with my teeth in the past.

Check out Tips #1-4

When I was young, my Dad took me
with him to his dental visit
'cause I was a bit scared to go.
Once I saw that everything went well,
There was no need to yell.

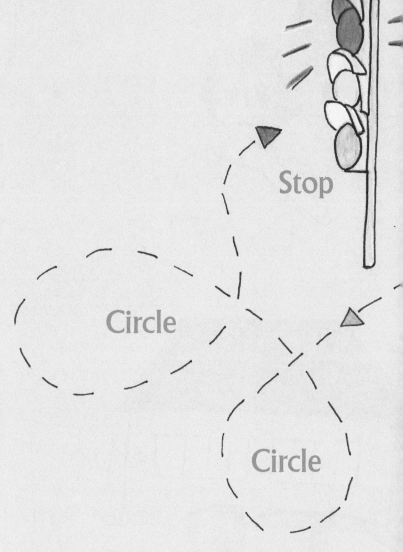

Stop

Circle

Circle

Follow with Your Finger:

The car goes left and then turns right
going up and down hills,
we circle and circle and of
course have to stop at the flashing,
brightly colored red light.

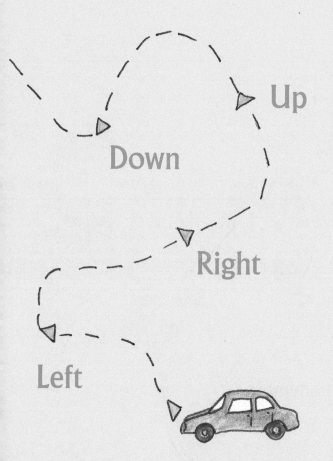

Up

Down

Right

Left

The seat belt hugs my body,
and I'm very relaxed.
It gets kind of bumpy over
the shiny metal train tracks.

In the waiting room, there are magazines, and cool pictures on the wall.

I even see a neat kids' chair shaped like a big, round soccer ball.

Colorful toys are piled high on the floor.

This can't be too bad. I'm not so worried anymore.

My sister Abi asks if I want to play with
the red blocks and the big yellow school bus
next to the plastic drawer.

I say "Yes," so we play for a while until we hear our names called.
Oh no, it's that time; we can't play anymore.

The nice front office lady sits next to the plant behind
the frosted glass door. My Mom tells her I have SPD;
what bothers others a *little* affects me a lot *more*.

Her name is Marilyn and she really seems to care.
My only complaint is when she pats me on the head
it feels like she is pressing hard on my hair.

We walk down a long hall,
many clean rooms on either side.
This is it, the blue room,
no need to use a special key.
Oh no–I want to flee!

Nurse Nan, the dental hygienist,
enters the room with a colorful bow in her hair
and a white mask around her neck,
straps looped over her ears.

Check out
Tip #5

Show, Tell and Do: What Does a Dental Hygienist Do?

Page 23

As Nurse Nan says hello,
my "king chair" starts to rise. Oh no,
that is a huge surprise!
"Actually ... it's not so bad, guys."

8

The dentist will check your gums and every tooth
to make sure gums are healthy and teeth are cavity free.
I'll turn on the overhead light on the count of three."

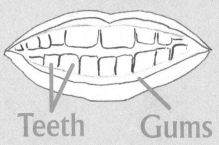

Teeth   Gums

The overhead light is very bright,

so the nurse gives me a neat pair

of dark blue glasses to wear.

They match my shirt

And they don't poke the backs of my ears!

She then puts a bib on me. "I'm not a baby," I say.

The nurse says, "I know! You're a big, strong, brave boy today."

The chain that holds the bib on my neck is kind of cold,

but it warms within a sec. Keeps my shirt clean without a speck.

Nurse Nan asks me to choose

a special flavor of toothpaste

that I'd like her to use.

So many choices–strawberry, melon, berry, and mint!

Strawberry

Melon

Berry

Mint

Check out
Tip #6

Smell the Toothpaste

Page 24

Guess which flavor I chose?

I'll let you in on a little secret:

it rhymes with "hint."

You guessed it–mint!

"If something annoys me," I ask,

"should I let you guys know?"

"Of course, Sam—your comfort matters.

We'll pause when you say so."

Pause

In

Go

Out

I breathe in and out and in and out, as my mom says.

It helps me to relieve inner stress.

I believe her ... I guess.

I sit very still as Nurse Nan
carefully cleans each tooth with
a white electric toothbrush.
It tickles my teeth as it scrubs.
She says, "Shiny!" I blush.

The cool water sprays in my mouth.
"Swish, swish, swish," says Nurse Nan.
"Mr. Thirsty," the plastic straw,
takes the water away.
I say to Nurse Nan, "Smart game plan!"

Check out
Tips #7 and 8

7 - Brushing the Correct Way

8 - Best Oral Hygiene

Page 24

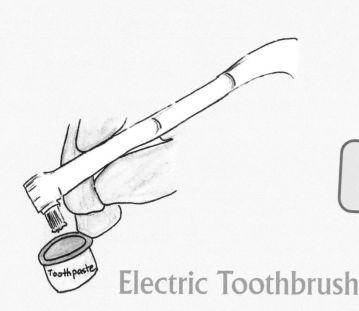

Toothpaste

Electric Toothbrush

Nurse Nan is quite helpful as she
shows me how to floss teeth
top and bottom, the correct way.
"Used floss is trashed," I say.

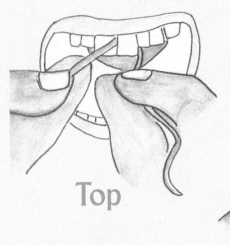

Top

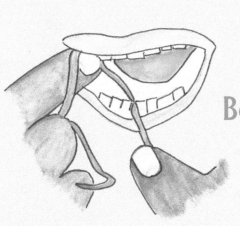

Bottom

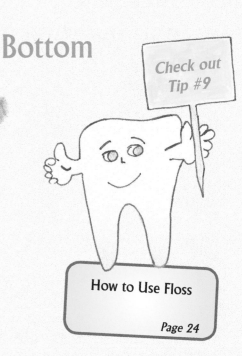

Check out
Tip #9

How to Use Floss

Page 24

I rub my tongue on my clean teeth.
Nurse Nan says they look great.
"The dentist will come in, so please
stretch during the short wait."

Dr. Bryan enters the room
wearing a white lab coat.
He greets me with a big smile
and asks me to open
my mouth wide for a little while.

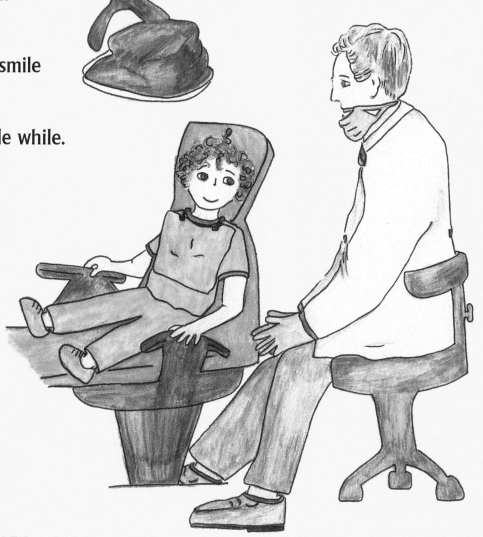

"How are you doing, Sam?" Dr. Bryan asks me
as he sits in the swivel chair next to mine.
I say, "Doing fine."
Nurse Nan takes her time to clean and floss.
After all, she said ... today ... "I am the boss!"

14

"Why are you wearing gloves?" I ask.

Dr. Bryan says, "It stops the germs from spreading;

some germs can make us very sick."

I reply, "Pretty slick."

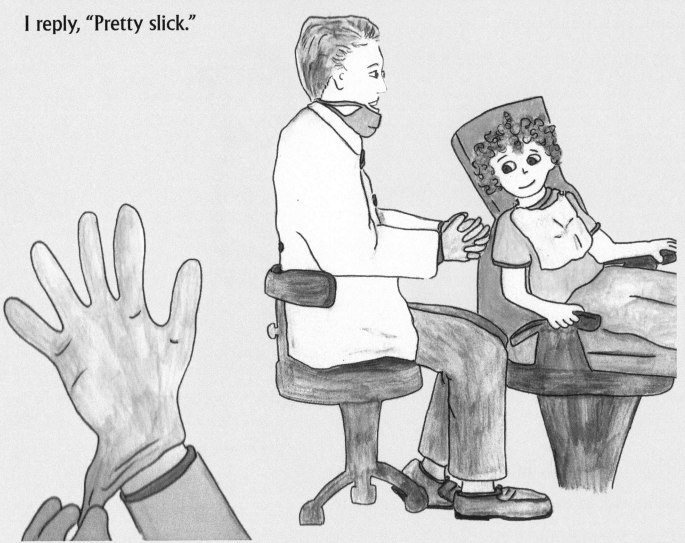

Dr. Bryan explains treatments through my dental exam
exactly like a show-tell-do and says, "Understand, Sam?"

There are lights and noises,
powerful-sounding dental tools.
There is scraping that kind
of gives me the chills up my spine.

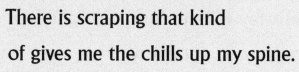

Check out
Tips #10 and 11

10 - Foods to Avoid

11 - All about Cavities

Page 25

"Oh no, that tooth hurts me,"
I say. He checks it carefully.
It may be a cavity.

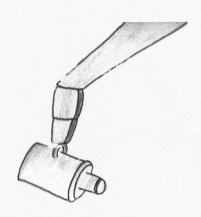

"Let's be sure," Dr. Bryan says.

"I will take an x-ray."

"The x-ray will not hurt me, right?"

"No Sam, do not worry.

All you need to do is bite real tight."

"This digital x-ray machine will
take a picture of your tooth,
in the blink of an eye.
Stay nice and still
and we can do it in one try."

The machine makes a noise
only I am able to hear;
because of having SPD,
I have sensitive ears.

Check out
Tips #12
and 13

12 - Photo of Your Teeth

13 - Fun Games to Play for Distraction

Page 25

He gives my cheek a little pinch
and a wiggle. Soon my mouth is numb.
I didn't even flinch!

He points out a cavity
in my tooth on the x-ray.
"With Nurse Nan's help,
we will clean it
and we'll fill it right away."

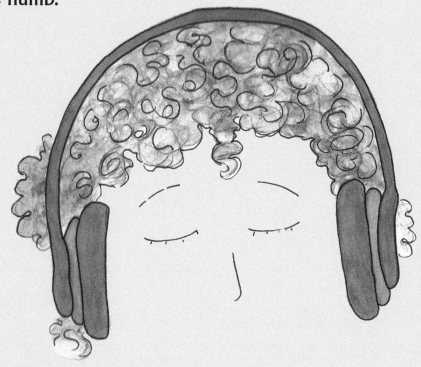

I have my headset on,
and I relax. Before the second
song plays, he says, "All done!"

I am happy now; my dental exam's a breeze.
And it's time for Mom, sis, and me to leave.

My cavity is filled.
My teeth are super clean: white and bright.
We leave the office with
a goodie bag sealed tight.

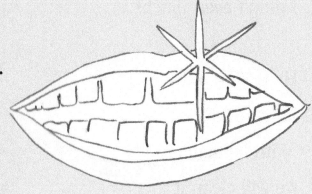

In the bag–a toothbrush,
toothpaste, minty floss,
and some kids' berry mouthwash.

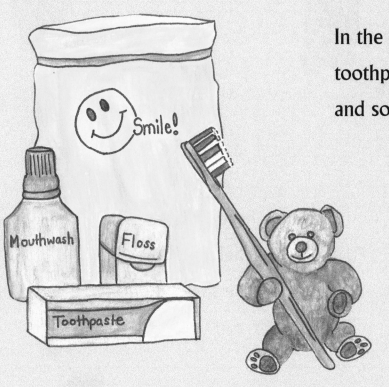

I notice something extra
at the bottom of the bag.
It's a bear, a kind of a cute teddy.
Wow, I want to name him
Fantastic, Furry, Fun Freddy!

As we walk to the front,

my sister asks Dr. Bryan,

"Do I have to brush my teeth?"

He responds with a smile,

"Only the ones you want to keep!"

That makes us laugh a while.

Mom schedules our next

visit, six months away, at nine.

What a fun time at the dentist!

Next time, I'll do just fine.

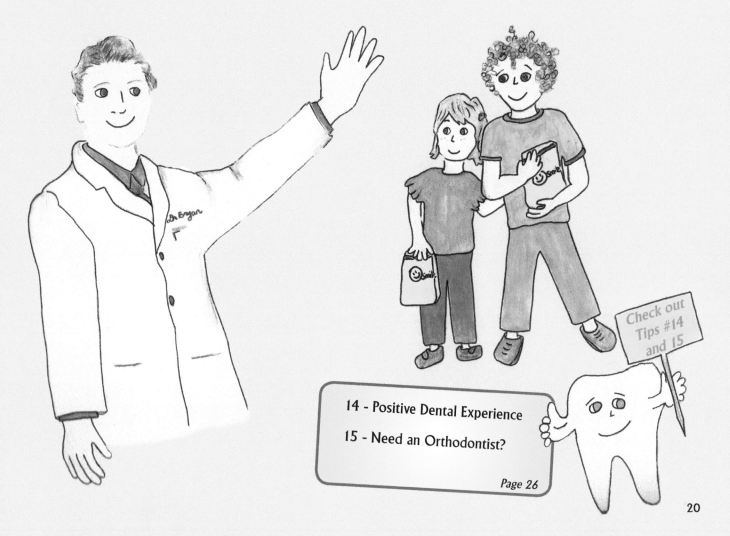

Check out Tips #14 and 15

14 - Positive Dental Experience

15 - Need an Orthodontist?

Page 26

Tips

#1
Telling Your Child about the Dentist

We ask parents to be very generic in telling their young children they have a dental appointment and that a dentist helps kids clean and check their teeth. For children under the age of six, we schedule first appointments in the morning. Generally, parents send in the child's health history forms prior to the appointment, which allows us to review any possible medical challenges or concerns and identify any nicknames. In addition, we educate parents to share with their children that the dentist and his staff are super nice and friendly. - Bryan D. Fisch, DDS

#2
Importance of Baby Teeth

Healthy baby teeth play a crucial role in the development of your child's jawbones and facial structures. Brush your child's teeth twice a day for at least two minutes, especially prior to bedtime, brushing every surface of each tooth, the gum line, and the tongue. A primary concern should be the comfort of your child at the dentist's office. You want your child to develop oral habits that will last a lifetime. A good start is to choose a dentist who will provide excellent dental care, treat your child with respect, and work with your child in an age-appropriate manner. Asking for a recommendation from friends, family members, or your pediatrician can be helpful. - Scott A. Kissinger, DDS

#3
When Should I Bring My Child to the Dentist?

Children are born with 20 baby teeth and then 32 adult teeth. The question we get asked the most is, "When should I start bringing my child to the dentist?" Our response is to bring them as early as teeth start coming in.

At our office, we accommodate each patient's specific needs. We offer "laughing gas" (nitrous oxide), headphones and music, TV and movies, comfy blankets, and simple techniques to provide distraction. For example, to distract a patient who is receiving anesthetic, we might have the assistant brush the patient's eyebrow with a finger. - Brian J. Svoboda, DDS

#4
New Teeth

When a baby's first teeth erupt, it's an exciting time. Usually starting with the lower front teeth (incisors), these teeth will sometimes erupt with much fanfare and fussiness and sometimes a mixture of wonder and excitement. If your child is a fussy teether, many remedies exist. Frozen teething rings, wet washcloths, and even large pieces of frozen carrot (being mindful of choking concerns) may provide some relief. Be careful with numbing medications that contain benzocaine, as the U.S. Food and Drug Administration recently warned that a rare side effect can result in your child's blood having a reduced ability to carry oxygen. That being said, a lot of parents report limited results with this method, as the numbing gels tend not to stay in the area in which they are applied.

At an average age of six, kids begin to lose their baby teeth and get new permanent replacements. Again, the lower incisors are usually the first to fall out and get replaced. Unfortunately, some kids' permanent teeth are too eager and erupt before the baby teeth fall out. Do not worry–your child is not part shark. As long as the baby teeth are loose and seem to be getting looser, you are probably pretty safe in wiggling the baby tooth until it comes out. Sometimes it is necessary to get the dentist involved to "help nature along." Consult your dentist if there isn't much progress. Around the same time, kids have permanent molars that erupt behind all the baby teeth and don't replace anything. Make sure to keep these "6-year molars" clean, because we need to keep them for the rest of our lives! - Daniel Nobel, DDS

#5
Show, Tell and Do: What Does a Dental Hygienist Do?

When starting treatment, we show the child we are placing a mask over our nose and mouth, and we say, "Don't forget, it is still Dr. Fisch behind this mask." Everything with children is "show, tell, and do," so there are few surprises. We always pick up our intra-oral camera and take a snapshot of the child and the parent(s) first and display this photo on the screen in front of the child. We might then ask the child to make a silly face and photograph that, too. Children love to see their own photos. Then, if the parents request a copy, we can e-mail it to them. - Bryan D. Fisch, DDS

A dental hygienist cleans the patient's teeth and talks with the patient about any dental concerns she may have. The hygienist also works closely with the dentist to ensure that the patient maintains good oral health. - Scott A. Kissinger, DDS

#6
Smell the Toothpaste

When we are about to polish children's teeth, we always allow them to smell the special toothpaste first–the one they selected. Then we take the prophy angle-polishing cup and spin it for them, so they can see the movement with the toothpaste tucked inside. - Bryan D. Fisch, DDS

#7
Brushing the Correct Way

Proper tooth brushing takes about 2-3 minutes. Modern electronic toothbrushes have a built-in timer to help. Using a soft-bristled toothbrush, start by brushing the outer surfaces of all upper teeth, followed by the outer surfaces of the lower teeth. Next, brush the inner surfaces of the upper teeth, followed by the inner surfaces of the lower teeth. Pay particular attention to the gum line by tilting the toothbrush at a 45-degree angle against the gum line. Finally, brush the chewing surfaces of all the teeth and the top of the tongue. - Scott A. Kissinger, DDS

#8
Best Oral Hygiene

The best ways to maintain oral hygiene in children are brushing the correct way, flossing, and rinsing with mouthwash. Make sure each tooth gets "brushed" in a circular motion and pattern. Start in the same area every night and end at the same area of the mouth every night. - Brian J. Svoboda, DDS

#9
How to Use Floss

Use about 18 inches of dental floss. By using about 2-3 inches of floss at a time, gently insert the floss between the teeth. Using an up-and-down sweeping motion, follow the curved contours of the teeth and below the gum line. - Scott A. Kissinger, DDS

#10
Foods to Avoid

Foods to avoid are sugary foods and drinks. Water is the best drink if possible, but anything in moderation is fine. If children do drink sugary drinks, make sure they brush their teeth before bed. Foods that strengthen the teeth are ones with fluoride, which helps protect the enamel and make it stronger. Calcium and potassium are both great for the body and teeth. - Brian J. Svoboda, DDS

#11
All about Cavities

Cavities are created by acids that are produced by bacteria that we have in our mouths and the sugars in foods we eat. The more we eat snacks high in sugar content, the more often we are exposing our teeth to the formation of cavities. Choosing foods like milk, cheese, meats, and nuts are better for our oral health than candies, cookies, cakes, potato chips, and dried fruits. - Scott A. Kissinger, DDS

#12
Photo of Your Teeth

We have our young patients focus on the computer monitor in front of them and look for the "picture of their teeth appearing on the screen." This helps them take their mind off of the digital x-ray sensor in their mouths. We show the small sensor to them first and allow them to touch it and experience how smooth it is. It then goes into a clear plastic sleeve that the children can touch prior to placing it in their mouths. - Bryan D. Fisch, DDS

#13
Fun Games to Play for Distraction

We play a leg-lift game with our patients prior to giving them an injection. We challenge them to see who can lift their legs, holding them together, straight off the chair and keeping them raised (at about a 40-degree angle) for a prize. This engages their abdominal muscles, distracts their brains from the actual injection, and requires them to focus for a few seconds, which allows us to give injections while they are distracted. We explain to them that we have to place a small amount of sleepy juice for the tooth while they are holding up their legs, and presto, the tooth and cheek are becoming numb! - Bryan D. Fisch, DDS

#14
Positive Dental Experience

It is important for the dentist to recognize, assess, and respond to the unique needs of all patients for that patient to have a positive dental experience. The dentist will talk with the patient about any concerns or fears she may have and help provide ways that the patient can comfortably have her dental needs taken care of. - Scott A. Kissinger, DDS

#15
Need an Orthodontist?

Our practice uses the "tell, show, and do" principle. Children have a strong tactile sense, so we allow children to handle an expander, wire, and brace, prior to these objects going into the mouth. We find that taking things slower is very helpful, especially with patients who have sensory challenges–perhaps we will change the upper wire at one visit instead of both upper and lower wires at once. We keep a child with the same assistant if possible, to enhance that child's comfort level and keep her anxiety to a minimum. In addition, we give a TON of positive feedback and encouragement at every visit. - Gary Holt, DDS, PC

Thanks to all the gifted and generous dentists listed below

Bryan D. Fisch, D.D.S., Alex G. Mizraji, D.D.S.

www.venturasmile.com

Ventura Center for Dental Health

2807 Loma Vista Road, Suite. 201

Ventura, CA 93003

Phone: (805) 653-5606

Stephen D. Barker, D.D.S., Scott A. Kissinger, D.D.S., Brian J. Svoboda, D.D.S.

www.southbridgedentistry.com

Southbridge Dentistry

7889 S. Lincoln Court, Suite 202

Littleton, CO 80122

Phone: (303) 798-4967

Daniel Nobel, D.D.S.

www.sunnysmilesdental.com

Sunny Smiles Dentistry for Children and Young Adults

789 S. Victoria Avenue, Suite 204

Ventura, CA 93003

Phone: (805) 644-5516

Gary Holt, D.D.S., P.C. Personalized Orthodontics

www.drgaryholt.com

4185 E. Wildcat Reserve Pkwy #100

Highlands Ranch, CO 80126

Phone: (303) 738-3175

Stories and Solutions

Every child is unique, and many people have a difficult time visiting the dentist. Here are some helpful stories, solutions, and tips from parents, professionals, and sensory kids about what works best for them. We all have something to teach one another. Maybe you'd like to share your own dental stories on my Web site: *www.sensitivesam.com.*

Gavin Bollard, parent
Sydney, Australia
http://life-with-aspergers.blogspot.com

Going to the dentist is a nightmare for us. Funny enough, my son with high-functioning autism handles it very well, but my son with Asperger's syndrome, attention-deficit disorder, and nonverbal learning disability is the one who panics. We go to special-needs dentists, but they still can't get near his mouth. If he needs major work, he needs to be put entirely under anesthesia, or he will endanger himself. In fact, we have problems getting him to clean his teeth ... and to this day (he's 12½), we still haven't been able to let the hairdresser use the electric razor on him because of the noise and vibration.

What affects him at the dentist? Basically, everything.

- Any discussion of the dentist
- Scary photos of teeth they have there, in the surgery section
- Loud noises, electronic noises and vibrations, drills, the sucker device, bright lights, shiny sharp instruments
- Scratchy feeling of things in his mouth
- Itchy feeling of glasses on his face
- Fluoride smell and rough texture and minty taste of glues and pastes
- Dental staff masks

Julie Clark, author of *Asperger's in Pink*
http://julieclarkart.blogspot.com

When looking for a dentist, we start by calling the office, trying to discern their level of familiarity with clients who have similar concerns as our daughter does, as well as their willingness to work with kids like her. We also talk a little about our daughter's sensory world prior to her first visit. Talking over the phone is only part of the process. One dentist sounded good "on paper," but was impatient and gruff in practice. We're fortunate that we've found a dental practice that is a solid fit. Here are a few tips to help you and your child have a more positive experience:

- Ask the staff to explain the process to your child beforehand, at each visit, so she knows which step is coming and how it may feel, taste, or smell to her.
- If your child is sensitive to certain tastes, ask about the flavors of toothpaste that will be used during the visit. Does she dislike mint? Ask for a substitute. Most dentists will be happy to comply.
- Choose to wait in the waiting room when your child is taken to the back room for his examination. Really. (Speak to the staff ahead of time.) Sometimes our kids will rise to the occasion if we are not present. It's a great step toward independence, isn't it?
- If the fluoride treatment can be given to your child in different forms, make sure to let your child select the one that will be the least invasive to her (yet effective).
- Be kind and patient. The dentist's office can be a scary place.

When your child complains about the pain she feels from the x-rays, listen to her. There may not be another solution, but the process can be very painful to the gums and sides of the mouth for people with sensory sensitivities.

Britt Collins, MS, OTR, coauthor of *Sensory Parenting: Newborns to Toddlers* and *Sensory Parenting: The Elementary Years*
www.sensoryparenting.com

Don't worry! There are things you can do to help your child prepare for the dentist.

- Get your child moving! Movement is very important, so make sure before a stressful event (and every day) you are providing your child with opportunities to run, jump, crash, swing, climb, and more.
- Heavy-work activities, such as pushing, pulling, doing wheelbarrow walks and wall handstands, and chewing crunchy and chewy foods can also help your child stay in a happy, calm state.
- Provide calming strategies before, during, and after the dentist, like drinking through a straw, taking deep breaths, blowing a cotton ball across the table, doing squishes on your child's shoulders and arms, and playing calming music in the car on the way there to help regulate your child's nervous system to that "just-right" state for tolerating a stressful situation.
- Have a surprise for your child when she is done, and praise your child for doing a good job!

Lisa Davis, MPH, creator, host, and producer of "It's Your Health Network," co-host of "Naturally Savvy Radio," and producer/co-host of "Beauty Inside Out," heard on national public and commercial radio *www.itsyourhealthnetwork.com* and *www.naturallysavvy.com*
"Beauty Inside Out" is heard on *www.radiomd.com*

I wanted to wait until my daughter with sensory issues (she is sensory defensive) was a teenager before I took her to the dentist, but I knew that wasn't a good idea. I took her at age 3. Oddly enough, she didn't mind us brushing her teeth, but she absolutely HATED to be tipped back, which is what happens when you go to the dentist.

When we arrived, we wanted to wait outside, since the waiting room was crowded and there was a TV blaring. The staff was understanding. A nice dental hygienist talked with us prior to going in. I told him how my daughter hated being tilted back. Once inside, they asked us to wait in the waiting room while they took my daughter into the exam room. I was not happy about this, but they said I should trust them. So, I waited, and then my daughter's screaming began. I was livid. I told them I should be in there with her. Believe it or not, things ended on a positive note. The screaming subsided, and the rest of the visit was fine. They took her photo (which she also hates because of the flash), and she got to pick out a balloon, which she loved.

Five years later, my daughter looks forward to going to the dentist. She even likes to play dentist at home! Open wide!

I wanted to be sure to have the best possible outcome, so here is what I did to prepare:

- Ask for references from an occupational therapist or parents who have children with similar issues; they may know a dentist who is sensitive to children with sensory issues. I called around and asked if the dentist was familiar with sensory issues. If they had no idea what I was talking about, I thanked them for their time and continued the search for a dentist and dental office that understood.
- Read about going to the dentist.
- Bring a favorite toy or blanket.
- Push for what you think is best. Make sure both staff and dentist are understanding and on board.
- Ask to visit the dentist's office prior to the appointment and talk to the staff in person.

Lorna and Pierrette d'Entremont
Sentio Life Solutions, Ltd, Developers of KidCompanions Chewelry
www.kidcompanions.com

KidCompanions Chewelry can make going to the dentist easier. It:

- Redirects anxious thoughts and uses pent-up energy by requiring the child to use the strong jaw muscles to chew and bite safely on this safe alternative instead of nonedibles or grinding the teeth.
- Provides comfort when holding on to the familiar KidCompanions Chewelry for the transition to the dentist's office and has a pendant to use as a hand fidget toy to relieve stress and anxiety while sitting in the dentist's chair.
- Can bring comfort to children and bring peace of mind to parents. It is an efficient sensory oral-motor tool that is free of phthalates (BPA), metals, and latex. This discreet chew necklace for sensory needs is made with U.S. Food and Drug Administration-approved materials, is CE marked, and is mom and occupational therapist recommended. It's also available from the same company that makes SentioCHEWS, which are made with a novel, highly resilient material that is more durable than products made of generic silicone.

Carrie Goldman, author of *Bullied: What Every Parent, Teacher, and Kid Needs to Know about Ending the Cycle of Fear*

Prior to visiting the dentist, I had my daughter practice brushing and spitting out toothpaste and chatted about the dentist. She chewed on therapeutic chewy tubes to help strengthen her jaw, so her mouth wouldn't feel so fatigued when she had to hold it open for extended amounts of time. We practiced putting silverware utensils in her mouth so she could prepare for foreign objects. She held her lovie.

Despite all of the preparation, there was a period of about 2 years when dentist visits were very grueling. We comforted her by letting her know that examinations don't last very long—usually only 30 minutes—and we had her watch her older sister get her teeth cleaned first. We explained that good cleanings help prevent the need for longer dental visits, so if she could tolerate one visit as best as possible, it might reduce the need for additional visits.

Connie Hammer, LMSW, and PCI-certified Parent Coach
Parent Coaching for Autism
www.parentcoachingforautism.com

With a client of mine, we extended social stories to "social poetry." We came up with the idea of writing the social story in rhyme because her son liked repetition of words with a similar sound. We condensed his social story into a poem that he memorized. Mom discovered that it helped him predict what would happen and calmed him when he recited it at the dentist's office.

Jennifer A. Janes
jenniferajanes.com

It's imperative to remember that the way we think our children will respond to a visit to the dentist may be completely different from what actually happens. You can't ever predict what a child with SPD will do from one moment to the next—whether your child will be under- or oversensitive to something. The unpredictability of SPD was made very real to me when my daughter had her first cavity filled.

She and I both dreaded the experience. I thought it would be a complete disaster, although it turned out very differently. At the dentist, they explained the basic procedure in a kid-friendly way, and they were careful to not specifically mention "drilling" or things that might frighten her unnecessarily. Because her cavity was so small, she didn't have to get a shot. The gas was sufficient. What none of us anticipated was the fact that she giggled through the entire session, as the gas relaxed her, and the vibrations of the drill actually tickled!

My recommendations to other families who take a sensory-sensitive child to the dentist are:

- Find a dentist who understands SPD and is willing to work with you and your child.
- Stay positive about the situation when speaking with or around your child, even if you're not as confident as you sound.
- Be aware that the situation could go better than you dreamed, or things could go south quickly. No matter what happens, you have to be able to respond quickly and calmly.

Carol Stock Kranowitz, MA, author of *The Out-of-Sync Child* and *The Goodenoughs Get in Sync* and coauthor of *In-Sync Activity Cards*

In-sync activities to do while at the dentist's office:

RUBBER BAND FUN

What you need: Assorted rubber bands and square plastic food container

What to do:
- Sort rubber bands by color, width, and length
- Make rubber band "rings" on all your fingers
- Half-hitch some together for a necklace
- Stretch rubber bands over the square container and pluck them like tiny guitar strings

PAPER AND PENCIL GAMES

What you need: Pad and pencils

What to do:

- Play Hangman
- Think of a long word, like "Establishment" or "Regeneration." Write the word at the top of a paper. Think of as many words as you can by rearranging the letters of the big word, and write them down.
- Fold a paper from top to bottom. Fold it again. You will have a rectangle. Open the folds. You and your mom are going to take turns drawing a goofy person. You start: In the top fold, draw a goofy head. Add a neck that goes down a bit into the second fold. Fold back the head so that all Mom can see is the neck. Then she attaches a body to the neck and draws the tops of legs in the third fold. In the third fold, you draw funny legs. Draw lines into the fourth fold for ankles and let Mom add the feet. Now unfold your silly person.

Bonnie Kimpling-Kelly, president of A.C.T. Now, Ltd, and Program Director of the P.A.T.H. Academy for Autism
www.autismbehavioranalyst.com

After two unsuccessful visits to the dentist, I read social stories to my son about going to the dentist daily for a month before his next appointment. When we got there and he got to the chair, he said, "Now Mommy, you go wait in the waiting room!" Then when the dentist called me in to see his cavity, my son pointed to the waiting area and said, "Ok, Mom–waiting room." SUCH a difference!

Terri Mauro, author of *50 Ways to Support Your Child's Special Education* and *The Everything Parent's Guide to Sensory Integration Disorder* *About.com children with special needs*

Most children don't exactly look forward to a visit to the dentist, but children with special needs may react with particular terror and misbehavior. If dental appointments are endless battles for you, your child, and your tooth-care provider, try these tactics for making exams less torturous for all concerned:

- Use a pediatric dentist
- Find a good hygienist

- Teach your child what to expect
- Pick a low-stress, high-success time for the appointment
- Prepare for waiting
- Keep dental care going all year
- Mind your own mouth

For more details, please visit *http://specialchildren.about.com/od/specialsituations/bb/dentist.htm*

Brian Mengini, parent
http://afatherslove.co

At an early age, Dominic was very sensory defensive in many regards. As a result, a tooth brushing was an uncomfortable task for him. This caused major issues with regard to his dental hygiene. We had to see a specialist about his teeth as they became sore and sensitive, and his mouth was in constant pain.

At the dentist, we learned that he had cavities on ten teeth and would have to get them filled. *He was three*. At a pre-filling appointment, we learned that his cavities were so far gone that he would need caps–simple fillings were not enough, and he had to be put under anesthesia.

Over the years, in part due to not wanting to have to have surgery again and in part being able to work past the tactile defensiveness, Dominic did much better with taking care of his teeth and easing the anxiety of the dentist. The little trinkets from the "treasure chest" at the dentist's office made the visit fun.

Jackie Linder Olson, coauthor of the *Sensory Parenting* series for Sensory World
www.SensoryParenting.com

Rewards! My son got a new game of his choice before going to the dentist. He could open it or start playing it on the way there. This strategy worked better than waiting till after the appointment to give it to him. Before, when he had to wait to get it, he would get so worked up that he would not care about the reward at the end of the appointment. But, having the reward on way there made him happy and at ease.

For us, the best things have been:

- Watching YouTube videos of going to the dentist.
- Sitting on me during his appointment when he was really little, around two.
- Finding one hygienist my son is comfortable with to clean his teeth. She's very sweet and tells him stories to distract him. He won't let the others near him.
- Lots of praise. The dentist and staff make a big deal about how great his teeth look and let him pick out a toothbrush. It definitely helps to have a super kid-friendly office with toys and stickers.

Bobbi Sheahan, author of *What I Wish I'd Known about Raising a Child with Autism*

The biggest mistakes I made–and what I'd caution others about, include:

- Thinking that a busy pediatric dental office with lots of toys and stimulation had any possibility of working.
- Not clarifying up front–really, really clarifying–how one of my kids has different needs.

Learn from my experience:

- Meet the dentist and the staff who will be interacting with your children.
- For appointments, familiarity and brevity are both very helpful, as is going when it's not busy.
- Avoid professionals who voice the opinion that your child's challenges–sensory issues, as well as dental imperfections–are evidence of poor character on your child's part or poor parenting on yours. Yes, you will encounter them. No, you do not need to put up with them.

My daughter really struggles with brushing her teeth, and we have worked very hard over the years to get her away from sweet drinks and sugary stuff, because that's all she would consume if we let her.

We've tried the pediatric dental equivalent of Disneyland, which was overwhelming for all of us, and we have long since settled upon the nice, calm, predictable office with the staff who know us. They have been wonderful about acclimating our daughter slowly over the years, and they have candy at the end (I know, I know ... but it works).

My kids love reading the same books in the lobby every time we go. We don't try to do anything else on the days when we go to the dentist. We have some rituals on the way, and we always get the same hygienist.

Now, my daughter is nine, and her advice to other kids who, like her, don't want to go to the dentist, is this: "I would just tell them that they have to go to the dentist if they want their teeth to stay in their mouth."

Barbara Smith, MS, OTR/L, author of *From Rattles to Writing: A Parent's Guide to Hand Skills* *RecyclingOT.com*

I have heard stories of children bringing their service dogs to the dentist and having them lie right on top of them. The deep pressure and comfort help while the dentist works.

Some recommendations:
- Prepare the child with deep-pressure activities shortly before the visit.
- Ask the dentist to place the heavy lead x-ray shield over the child.
- Provide squeeze and fidget toys.
- Offer headphones with favorite music.
- Prepare a visual schedule.
- Do not dwell on the exam until the day of the visit, to lessen anxiety.
- Reinforce the visit with stickers, music, a video, or a visit to the playground—whatever works for your child.
- Prepare children with play-doll and dentist kits, where they are the dentist working on the child's teeth.
- Perhaps place her favorite doll in the dentist's chair, too.
- Some children do best with gradual exposure to the dentist's office.

When the child goes to the dentist, he experiences aversive touch. He has to keep his mouth open, which can be uncomfortable, and he may have difficulty processing directions like "Open more," "Open less wide," and so on, because these directions require body awareness, which may be decreased for him. The child may have difficulty processing the verbal directions. A child's brain interprets where his body is in space on the basis of the information he receives from his proprioceptive sensory receptors–in muscles and joints–and the vestibular receptors in the inner ear, which tell him how his body is moving in relation to the pull of gravity.

Children with SPD often have brains that are unable to organize. Sometimes, they don't know how to interpret movement and where they are in space. So the dentist may give a direction such as "Turn your head toward me," and the child will turn upward, instead. In addition, some types of SPD affect language processing skills so that the child has difficulties following both verbal and gestural directions. We may use pictures to communicate what the dentist wants the child to do, gesture instead of using words, or practice following the needed directions at home in advance. Perhaps the child will need a combination of gestural and visual directions. Creative problem solving will help determine which options work best to meet the specific child's needs.

Occupational therapists strive to help children by:

- Affecting the child's overall brain function through guided sensory activities during therapy
- Designing a sensory diet and training parents and teachers to implement it to help the child maintain a balance of alertness and calm
- Adapting to specific situations, such as going to the dentist

Gina St Aubin, editor, author, blogger, and advocate
Board of Directors, Sensory Processing Disorder Foundation
http://specialhappens.com

We made it through the waiting room, somehow. There was nothing special here. General kid-related items were scattered. Standard toys. Brightly colored plastic chairs against light colored, almost white walls; no warmth to be found. In the purely white and cold, sterile room that followed, we could feel the tension that threatened to explode from Jackson at any moment. We felt horrible, but we knew we had to be prepared to hold him ... struggle with him ... reassure him ... encourage him. After all, we had to know what was going on with his teeth. His teeth were green! His sensory issues alone leave teeth brushing to be less than complete. He can't do it ... doesn't do it. I do. His mouth tells him to wrap around the brush, and his head pushes away no matter how hard he tries, making it impossible to get the green off his teeth. He tries. He just can't. It's not his fault. He's working against his body, against his SPD.

So, needless to say, this and subsequent dental visits didn't go well. Fast forward. We find ourselves in a conversation with a family friend about dentists (their son has special needs). Beyond behavioral similarities, our boys both have

SPD. Our friend made a recommendation, and we decided to go for it—and everything was different. This dental office was warm, decorated with child-friendly themes ... not the tinny or cheesy kind, but the thoughtful kind. There was a room slightly separated from the main waiting area that had video stations with headphones. In an adjoining area were beanbag chairs and a TV. All the seating was comfortable. Everything was strongly colored, yet subtle—not sharp. The waiting area was separated with doors, and the very large patient area was just as warm, yet large. There were large fish tanks full of relaxing creatures. The rooms held all the equipment necessary for dental exams, and the lighting was soft, even dim at our entrance. The seating was a black leather dental chair, with rolling chairs for parents. On the ceiling were movies, with the headphones lying next to the headrest for Jackson. He was given a choice of movies. He was reassured throughout.

Everyone was patient ... even holding an air of unnecessity ... it wasn't dire to get him examined. It was more important, the staff said, that his experience be a positive one, that if he had to come back multiple times and work up to sitting in the chair, remaining calm and settled, trusting the dental staff, and completing an appointment, then that's what it would take.

The dental experiences were polar opposites. Everything about the second dental office was calming and tailored to ease the senses, without losing the ability to cater to children. The differences were not only in the decoration of the environment, but also in the equipment, which was provided in a thoughtful manner:

- A movie of his choosing to watch, strategically located.
- Headphones that block out any dental noises (like drills and "weird" words) and that bring the movie closer to home.
- Soft, comfortable furniture.
- Calming decor (including fish tanks).
- Well-trained staff.

All of it made the difference for that visit and our future visits. All told, when Jackson's sensory needs were addressed within the dental office, the visit to the dentist became a success.

Miss Speechie, licensed speech-language pathologist and author
http://speechtimefun.blogspot.com

I recommend using social stories to help introduce the idea of going to the dentist for the first time.

"A Social Story describes a situation, skill, or concept in terms of relevant social cues, perspectives, and common responses in a specifically defined style and format. The goal of a Social Story is to share accurate social information in a patient and reassuring manner that is easily understood by its audience. Half of all Social Stories developed should affirm something that an individual does well. Although the goal of a Social Story should never be to change the individual's behavior, that individual's improved understanding of events and expectations may lead to more effective responses."

–Carol Gray

Use pictures and scenarios, so children know what to expect. I had a student that needed a palate expander put in her mouth. I created a specific social story, using her name, the date she was going to the dentist for the expander, what to expect at the dentist, what exactly the expander did, how it would be put in, what needed to be completed by her parent, and, ultimately, the positive results from the use of the expander. In addition, I reassured my student that I would be there to help. It worked, and so did the expander!

Katie Yeh, mom, licensed and credentialed speech-language pathologist, creator and author of *Playing with Words 365*, and owner of Tiny Steps Speech Therapy
playingwithwords365.com
www.tinystepsspeechtherapy.com

Sometime in the early elementary years, children begin to lose their baby teeth in preparation for their adult teeth to grow in. For many kids, this is an exciting time for them! They see their peers lose their teeth and want to experience this phenomenon with their friends.

But, not all children like losing teeth. In fact, some children can become a bit embarrassed because of the holes in their mouths. On top of the physical changes that come with losing teeth, which can feel funny, this time can also come with some changes in the child's speech. Sometimes, when young children lose many of their front teeth around the same time, they can find it difficult to produce some speech sounds. Specifically, the production of the /s/ and /z/ sounds, which are produced by placing the tongue behind the front teeth, can be affected by this short-term change in dentition. Without the teeth there, some children may produce these sounds with a slight frontal lisp, which distorts the sounds and makes them sound more like the "th" sound. Though many children don't even notice this slight change in their speech, other children can be quite sensitive to these changes and may be reluctant to smile or even talk.

So what can you do, as a parent, if you find that your child is feeling embarrassed about his speech during this time of transition? Here are my tips, as a speech-language pathologist and mother of three:

- First, acknowledge your child's feelings. This is a very important first step in helping him become more comfortable during this transition.
- After you acknowledge your child's feelings, talk about how losing teeth is a normal part of growing up and that all of his or her friends will be losing their teeth, too! Talk about your child's friends at school and which ones have lost which teeth.
- Now that your child understands just how normal this all is and that he is not alone, you can address the speech changes he may be experiencing. Talk about how all his friends will have a time where they may talk a little differently because they are missing some teeth. See if your child can come up with examples of children in his class that talk a little differently. Usually children will start to feel better about these changes when they know they are not alone.
- Now, tell her the GREAT news that ... this will not last forever! Soon, adult teeth will grow in, and it will no longer feel weird. She will be able to once again say those sounds the right way!

For additional information, treatment, education, and advocacy on Sensory Processing Disorder, please visit: *http://spdnow.org.*

About the Author

Photo courtesy of McBoat Photography

Marla Roth-Fisch is a happily married mother of two, including a son with Sensory Processing Disorder (SPD). Marla is the creative award-winning author/illustrator of *Sensitive Sam Visits the Dentist.* In addition to participating in various activities and volunteer work with her family, Marla is an active board member at the STAR Institute for Sensory Processing Disorder. *Sensitive Sam*, her first award-winning children's book in the *Sensitive Sam* series, is available (www.SensitiveSam.com).

CPSIA information can be obtained
at www.ICGtesting.com
Printed in the USA
BVHW01s0141070718
520938BV00003B/12/P

9 780986 067303